ESCAPE FROM PLANET
ALCATRAZ

FLAMING FIELDS OF DEATH

BY MICHAEL DAHL

ILLUSTRATED BY SHEN FEI

STONE ARCH BOOKS
a capstone imprint

Escape from Planet Alcatraz is published by
Stone Arch Books
A Capstone Imprint
1710 Roe Crest Drive
North Mankato, Minnesota 56003
www.capstonepub.com

Library of Congress Cataloging-in-Publication Data
Names: Dahl, Michael, author. | Fei, Shen (Illustrator), illustrator.
Title: Flaming fields of death / by Michael Dahl ; illustrated by Shen Fei.
Description: North Mankato, MN : Stone Arch Books, a Capstone imprint,
   [2020] | Series: Escape from planet Alcatraz
Identifiers: LCCN 2019005605 (print) | LCCN 2019009643 (ebook) |
   ISBN 9781496583208 (eBook PDF) | ISBN 9781496583130
   (library binding)
Subjects: LCSH: Science fiction. | Prisons—Juvenile fiction. | Escapes—
   Juvenile fiction. | Extraterrestrial beings—Juvenile fiction. | Extrasolar
   planets—Juvenile fiction. | Adventure stories. | CYAC: Science fiction.
   | Prisons—Fiction. | Escapes—Fiction. | Extraterrestrial beings—
   Fiction. | Adventure and adventurers—Fiction. | LCGFT: Science
   fiction. | Action and adventure fiction.
Classification: LCC PZ7.D15134 (ebook) | LCC PZ7.D15134 Fl 2020
   (print) | DDC 813.54 [Fic]—dc23
LC record available at https://lccn.loc.gov/2019005605

Summary: Teenage friends Zak Nine and Erro, a young furling from the
planet Quom, are in a tough spot. The boys are lost in a huge field and
surrounded by bursts of flame and snakes that spit fire. Even worse is
the killer cyborg tank that is pursuing them. The boys must find a way to
survive if they ever hope to escape from the prison planet called Alcatraz.

Editor: Aaron J. Sautter
Designer: Kay Fraser
Production Specialist: Katy LaVigne

Design elements: Shutterstock: Agustina Camilion, A-Star, Dima Zel,
Draw_Wing_Zen, Hybrid_Graphics, Metallic Citizen

Printed and bound in the United States of America.
PA71

TABLE OF CONTENTS

ERRO

PLATEAU of LENG

PHANTOM FOREST

POISON SEA

VULCAN MOUNTAINS

LAKE of GOLD

METAL MOON

DIAMOND MINES

MONSTER ZOO

PITS of NO RETURN

PRISON
STRONGHOLDS

SWAMP of FLAME

SCARLET JUNGLE

PRISON
ENERGY DRIVES

SPACE PORT
PRISONER INTAKE

ABYSS of GIANTS

ZAK

THE PRISONERS

ZAK NINE

Zak is a teenage boy from Earth Base Zeta. He dreams of piloting a star fighter one day. Zak is very brave and is a quick thinker. But his enthusiasm often leads him into trouble.

ERRO

Erro is a teenage furling from the planet Quom. He has the fur, long tail, sharp eyes, and claws of his species. Erro is often impatient with Zak's reckless ways. But he shares his friend's love of adventure.

THE PRISON PLANET

Alcatraz... there is no escape from this terrifying prison planet. It's filled with dungeons, traps, endless deserts, and other dangers. Zak Nine and his alien friend, Erro, are trapped here. They had sneaked onto a ship hoping to see an awesome space battle. But the ship landed on Alcatraz instead. Now they have to work together if they ever hope to escape!

ZAK'S STORY... DANGEROUS FIELDS >>>

Last night Erro and I were running from an army of tanklike robots when a raging storm hit. Today we're hiding out in a field full of thick mud and tall grass. The robots are gone. But now a dangerous new enemy is tracking us through the grassy field....

>>>>

CHAPTER ONE:
FIRE AND CLAW

"What are those flames?" I ask my alien friend.

I can see blue fire shooting up from the ground nearby.

Erro pulls me down to hide in the tall grass. Our boots sink into the sticky mud.

"Shhh, it is coming," Erro whispers.

I don't see or hear anything.

But I know this kid from Quom can hear things I can't. It's those pointy ears of his.

RRRRUUMMMMMMBBLE!

The ground trembles and the tall grass shakes.

A giant tank suddenly comes into view, flashing its search light.

"Run!" I shout.

The cyborg tank is the most dangerous guard on Alcatraz.

The machine has laser guns, metal claws, and a human brain. Its brain sits in a plastic dome on top of the tank.

The giant treads are heading in our direction!

Erro and I try to race away. But it's not easy moving through the thick muck.

Then a claw reaches up from the mud and grabs my foot.

CHAPTER TWO:
THE ALIEN PILOT

I glance down and see a disgusting giant insect lying in the muck.

One of its claws is holding my foot.

"Help me!" says the creature in a buzzing voice.

"He is a Glamoran," says Erro.

"His people are friendly to the Quom."

That's a person? I think.

"My ship crashed not far from here,"
he says. "In the Igneous Quag."

"*Igneous Quag?* What's that?" I ask.

RRRRUUMMMMMMBBLE!

The deadly tank moves closer.

The insect alien sees the light
flashing and lets go of my foot.

"My ship," he wheezes. Then he
points. "That way! Run!"

"What about you?" Erro asks the insect alien.

"I'm hurt," the alien replies. "There's no time. Save yourselves—go!"

Erro and I race away. Our boots are sloshing through a foot of swamp water. The grinding treads of the tank grow louder.

Behind us, I hear a sickening crunch and a gurgling scream. The tank stops.

"Poor Glamoran," says Erro.

CHAPTER THREE:
FIRE AND WATER

We pause a moment in the thick grass and water.

Erro's yellow eyes gleam. "If there is a ship—" he begins.

"—we could use it to escape Alcatraz!" I say, finishing his thought.

But first, we have to find it.

ZZZZWWWOOOSH!

Suddenly a blue flame shoots up from the mucky water. It misses my foot by only a few inches!

ZZZZWWWOOOSH!

Another blue flame shoots up a few feet away.

ZZZZWWWOOOSH!

ZZZZWWWOOOSH!

Two more large flames shoot up close
to us—too close.

"This is what the Glamoran meant
by *Igneous Quag*," says Erro. "It must
mean 'fiery swamp.'"

"How do you know that?" I ask.

"I overheard some prisoners talking about it," he says. "This swamp lies above an old Alcatraz power station."

"That must be where the flames come from," I say.

"Not all of them," says Erro, pointing toward the water.

A huge, green snake circles around my boots. The snake opens its jaws, and a blast of yellow flame shoots out.

"Yow!" I shout, jumping back from the snake. "This place is a nightmare!"

I look and see more snakes swimming around us. They seem to be nibbling on the grass.

Several of the disgusting creatures lift their heads above the water. They stare at us with black eyes. Then they open their mouths wide.

SSSSAAAAAAAA!

The snakes start spitting fire at us! Erro and I jump back from the flames.

CHAPTER FOUR:
FLAMING DEAD END

The ground suddenly trembles again. The tank must be getting closer!

A deadly laser blast fires right above our heads.

THOOOOMMMM!

On the other side of a wide pool, something explodes.

"What's that?" I ask.

"The ship—the tank's laser took it out!" Erro shouts.

I can hear the tank crashing through the grass somewhere behind us.

We turn to run, but I slip in the mud and fall.

"Zak," says Erro. "Have you noticed what the serpents are eating?"

"I really haven't had the time!" I reply, wiping mud off my face.

Erro pulls up a dripping, purple weed. "They are only interested in these," he says.

"Forget the weeds!" I say. "The tank's coming for us!"

I grab Erro's paw, and he pulls me up. The cyborg tank is plowing toward us through the muck and water.

"Let's beat it!" I say.

But the tank shoots another laser blast just over our heads. The grass behind us bursts into flame.

We're trapped!

CHAPTER FIVE:
SNAKE BAIT

The tank rumbles toward us.

Suddenly Erro heads toward it! He half runs, half swims through the water.

"What are you doing?" I shout.

Erro runs up to one of the tank's treads. He starts shoving something between the wheels.

It's those stupid weeds. Erro is stuffing them into the tank's treads!

The tank moves closer, driving into the water. Dozens of snakes, maybe hundreds, are chasing the purple weeds.

The snakes spit fire as they swim between the tank's wheels and treads. A small explosion suddenly rips through the tank's wheels.

Erro looks at me with wide eyes. We know what comes next. We both duck down into the water.

KARRRROOOOOM!

The entire cyborg tank explodes! Snake bodies go flying through the air. Flaming chunks of metal fall into the water around us.

It's over. The tank is destroyed.

"That is for the Glamoran," says Erro softly.

I feel sad too. But we have to keep moving. More Alcatraz guards will soon be coming our way. . . .

GLOSSARY

cyborg (SY-bohrg)—a creature that is part human and part machine

dungeon (DUHN-juhn)—a prison, usually underground

igneous (IG-nee-uhss)—relating to fire or flames

laser (LAY-zur)—a thin, intense beam of light

muck (MUHK)—thick or slimy mud

quag (KWAG)—an area of wet, swampy land

serpent (SUR-pent)—a snake

species (SPEE-sheez)—a group of living things that share similar features

tread (TRED)—a strong metal belt that goes around a truck's or tank's wheels

TALK ABOUT IT

1. Zak and Erro see blue flames shooting up from the ground in the grassy field. Can you think of a similar place on Earth where fire shoots out of the ground? Where could you go to see this in real life?

2. The injured insectlike alien tells the boys to leave him behind. Why do you think he does this? If you were Zak or Erro, what would you do? Would you help the alien get to his ship?

3. The Swamp of Flame is filled with big, fire-spitting snakes. What other creatures might live in the fields? Do you think they all breathe fire like the snakes?

WRITE ABOUT IT

1. Erro's plan to defeat the cyborg tank worked, but it was risky. Write about a time when you took a risk to achieve something that seemed impossible. Describe how it made you feel at the time.

2. Use your imagination to design your own super cyborg tank. Write down the tank's features and weapons. Then write your own short story about the tank hunting and catching an escaped criminal on planet Alcatraz.

ABOUT THE AUTHOR

Michael Dahl is the author of more than 300 books for young readers, including the bestselling Library of Doom series. He is a huge fan of Star Trek, Star Wars, and Doctor Who. He has a fear of closed-in spaces, but has visited several prisons, dungeons, and strongholds, both ancient and modern. He made a daring escape from each one. Luckily, the guards still haven't found him.

ABOUT THE ILLUSTRATOR

Shen Fei loved comic books as a child. By the age of five he began making his own comic books and drawing scenes from his favorite movies. After graduating from art school he worked in the entertainment industry, creating art for film, games, and books. Shen currently lives in Malaysia and works as a freelance illustrator for publishers all over the world. He also teaches at a local art school as a guest lecturer.